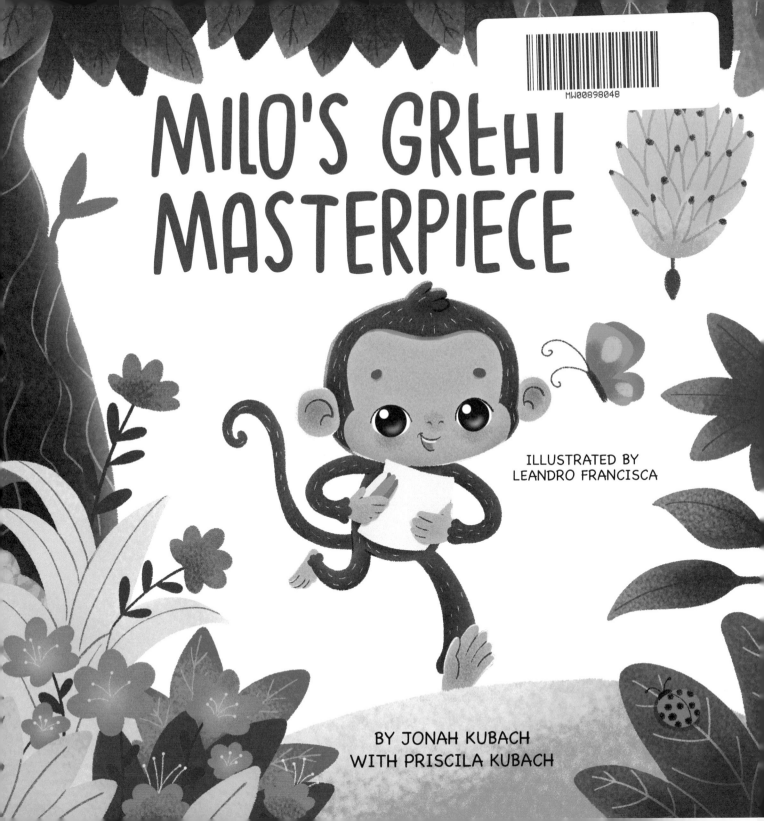

MILO'S GRЄΔT MASTERPIECE

ILLUSTRATED BY
LEANDRO FRANCISCA

BY JONAH KUBACH
WITH PRISCILA KUBACH

Created by Jonah Kubach, 7 years old, Florida Second Grader, this truly inspiring, gloriously-illustrated and funny story, will make your heart melt and put a smile on your face.

Jonah didn't always like to read or write, but once he put his mind into it, he thrived. Jonah wrote this story in one afternoon. With the help of his mom, they transformed his amazing story into a book. We are all so proud of him. We hope you enjoy it, as much as we did.

By Jonah Kubach with Priscila Kubach

"I can do all things through Christ who strengthens me" Philippians 4:13

In the heart of a vibrant jungle, where the trees were tall and the flowers bright, lived a happy little monkey named Milo.

Milo adored his mom and wanted to make her a special present. So, one bright morning, he decided he would draw her a picture, a portrait of his mom. It was going to be his best work ever, a true Masterpiece.

"It has to be perfect," he thought to himself, as he grabbed his crayons and paper. He worked on the picture all morning, carefully choosing colors and adding details. When he was done, he thought it looked good.

"Wow, this is really good."
Milo said out loud.

"But I wonder if it is perfect?" Milo thought to himself. "I really want this picture to be perfect for my mom. Maybe I can check with my friends. I am sure they can help me make it even better."

Milo decided to head off deep into the jungle to find some of his friends and get advice on his drawing.

Milo was feeling excited about sharing his picture with his friends as he swung from tree to tree deep into the jungle. And at last, he spotted some of his friends resting by the main pond.

First, Milo bumped into his friend Ella, the elephant, who was slurping some water from the pond. "Hey Ella, I'm making a portrait for my mom. Do you want to see it? Maybe you can help me make it perfect." Milo asked eagerly, showing her the picture. "Yes, I do." Ella chuckled softly, "Oh, Milo, I love this picture, but her ears look a little too small, maybe you could make them a little bigger? That would make it perfect." said Ella.

So he did.

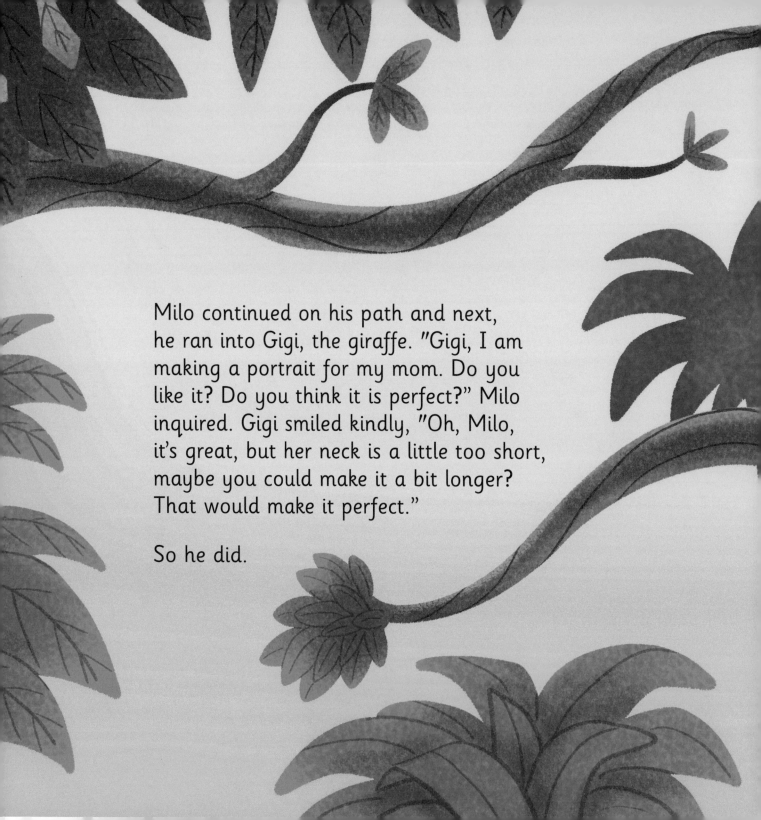

Milo continued on his path and next,
he ran into Gigi, the giraffe. "Gigi, I am
making a portrait for my mom. Do you
like it? Do you think it is perfect?" Milo
inquired. Gigi smiled kindly, "Oh, Milo,
it's great, but her neck is a little too short,
maybe you could make it a bit longer?
That would make it perfect."

So he did.

Milo happily trotted around the pond until he met Charles, the crocodile. "Charles, I am making a portrait for my mom. Do you like it? Do you think it is perfect?" Milo asked. Charles chuckled, "Milo, I do like it, but her mouth seems a little too small. Maybe you could make it a little bigger? That would make it perfect."

So he did.

Next, Milo saw his friend Zara, the zebra, walking up the hill. "Zara, I am making a portrait for my mom. Do you like it? Do you think it is perfect?" Milo wondered aloud. Zara giggled, "Milo, I like it a lot. But she doesn't have any stripes. Maybe you could add a few stripes in? That would make it perfect."

So he did.

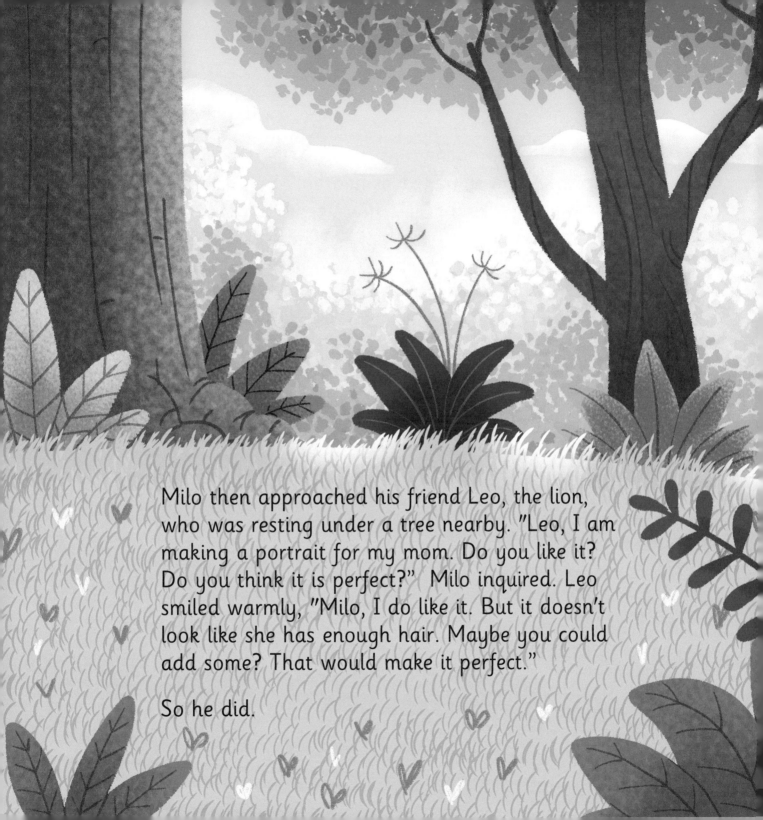

Milo then approached his friend Leo, the lion, who was resting under a tree nearby. "Leo, I am making a portrait for my mom. Do you like it? Do you think it is perfect?" Milo inquired. Leo smiled warmly, "Milo, I do like it. But it doesn't look like she has enough hair. Maybe you could add some? That would make it perfect."

So he did.

Lastly, Milo approached his friend Belle, the deer, who was nibbling on some leaves nearby. "Belle, I am making a portrait for my mom. Do you like it? I really want it to be perfect. What do you think?" Milo asked, excitement bubbling inside him. "Milo, it's lovely! Your mom looks so happy and full of life. You've portrayed her beautifully! But I noticed she is missing antlers, perhaps you could add a couple? That would make it perfect."

So he did.

With all the changes made, Milo felt ready. He was proud of his work even though he wasn't sure it looked perfect. He knew he had done his best, and that was what mattered most. With the help of his friends, he believed he had a great masterpiece on his hands.

He hurried home, excited to
give his gift to his mom.

"Mama, I made something special just for you!" Milo said, holding out the picture. "I made a portrait of you. I don't know if it is perfect, but I hope you like it!"

As Milo proudly showed her the portrait, his mom gasped... in delight.
And with her eyes wide open she said. "Oh, Milo! I can see you worked very hard on this drawing. I have always wanted a portrait like this!" Tears of happiness welled up in her eyes as she hugged Milo tightly.
"Thank you, my dear, I love it. It is absolutely perfect."

Milo beamed with pride, knowing that his picture, with a little help from his friends, made his mom's day truly special. He hugged his mom back and realized then that perfection isn't about flawless features, but about showing love. And Milo's portrait was perfect because it came straight from the heart, just like his love for his mom.

And with that, the little monkey and his mom went on their way, his heart full of love and pride, ready to share his masterpiece with the whole world.

THE END

A special thank you to everyone who has helped and supported us on this journey to get this book completed. You believed in us, "and so we did."

Made in the USA
Columbia, SC
21 November 2024